THE BLUE
BEHEMOTH

THE BLUE BEHEMOTH

by Leigh Brackett

Shannon's Imperial Circus was a jinxed space-carny leased for a mysterious tour of the inner worlds. It made a one-night pitch on a Venusian swamp-town—to find that death stalked it from the jungle in a tiny ball of flame.

Bucky Shannon leaned forward across the little hexagonal table. He knocked over the pitcher of *thil*, but it didn't matter. The pitcher was empty. He jabbed me in the breastbone with his forefinger, not very hard. Not hard enough to jar the ribs clean loose, just enough to spring them.

"We," he said, "are broke. We are finished, through. Washed up and down the drain." He added, as an afterthought, "Destitute."

I looked at him. I said sourly, "You're kidding!"

"Kidding." Shannon put his elbows on the table and peered at me through a curtain of very blond hair that was trying hard to be red. "He says I'm kidding! With Shannon's Imperial Circus, the Greatest Show in Space, plastered so thick with attachments...."

"It's no more plastered than you are." I was sore because he'd been a lot quicker grabbing the pitcher. "The Greatest Show in Space. Phooey! I've wet-nursed Shannon's Imperial Circus around the Triangle for eleven years, and I know. It's lousy, it's mangy, it's broken-down! Nothing works, from the ship to the roustabouts. In short, it stinks!"

I must have had the pitcher oftener than I thought. Nobody insults Buckhalter Shannon's Imperial Circus to Buckhalter Shannon's face unless he's tired and wants a long rest in a comfy fracture-frame.

Shannon got up. He got up slowly. I had plenty of time to see his grey-green eyes get sleepy, and hear the quarter-Earth-blood Martian girl wailing about love over by the battered piano, and watch the

5

slanting cat-eyes of the little dark people at the tables swing round toward us, pleased and kind of hungry.

I had plenty of time to think how I only weigh one-thirty-seven to Shannon's one-seventy-five, and how I'm not as young as I used to be.

I said, "Bucky. Hold on, fella. I...."

Somebody said, "Excuse me, gentlemen. Is one of you Mister Buckhalter Shannon?"

Shannon put his hands down on his belt. He closed his eyes and smiled pleasantly and said, very gently:

"Would you be collecting for the feed bill, or the fuel?"

I shot a glance at the newcomer. He'd saved me from a beating, even if he was a lousy bill-collecter; and I felt sorry for him. Bucky Shannon settled his shoulders and hips like a dancer.

The stranger was a little guy. He even made me look big. He was dressed in dark-green synthesilk, very conservative. There was a powdering of grey in his hair and his skin was pink, soft, and shaved painfully clean. He had the kind of a face that nice maiden-ladies will trust with their last dime. I looked for his strong-arm squad.

There didn't seem to be any. The little guy looked at Shannon with pale blue eyes like a baby, and his voice was softer than Bucky's.

He said, "I don't think you understand."

I felt cold, suddenly, between the shoulders. Somebody scraped a chair back. It sounded like he'd ripped the floor open, it was so quiet. I got my brassies on, and my hands were sweating. Bucky Shannon sighed, and let his fist start traveling, a long, deceptive arc.

Then I saw what the little guy was holding in his hand.

I yelled and knocked the table over into Bucky. It made a lot of noise. It knocked him sideways and down, and the little dark men jumped up, quivering and showing their teeth. The Martian girl screamed.

6

Bucky heaved the table off his lap and cursed me. "What's eating you, Jig? I'm not going to hurt him."

"Shut up," I said. "Look what he's got there. Money!"

The little guy looked at me. He hadn't turned a hair. "Yes," he said. "Money. Quite a lot of it. Would you gentlemen permit me to join you?"

Bucky Shannon got up. He grinned his pleasantest grin. "Delighted. I'm Shannon. This is Jig Bentley, my business manager." He looked down at the table. "I'm sorry about that. Mistaken identity."

The little guy smiled. He did it with his lips. The rest of his face stayed placid and babyish, almost transparent. I realized with a start that it wasn't transparent at all. It was the most complete dead-pan I ever met, and you couldn't see into those innocent blue eyes any more than you could see through sheet metal.

I didn't like him. I didn't like him at all. But he had money. I said, "Howdy. Let's go find a booth. These Marshies make me nervous, looking like hungry cats at a mouse-hole."

The little guy nodded. "Excellent idea. My name is Beamish. Simon Beamish. I wish to—ah—charter your circus."

*

I looked at Bucky. He looked hungrier than the Marshies did. We didn't say anything until we got Beamish into a curtained booth with a fresh pitcher of *thil* on the table. Then I cleared my throat.

"What exactly did you have in mind, Mr. Beamish?"

Beamish sipped his drink, made a polite face, and put it down. "I have independent means, gentlemen. It has always been my desire to lighten the burden of life for those less fortunate...."

Bucky got red around the ears. "Just a minute," he murmured, and started to get up. I kicked him under the table.

7

"Shut up, you lug. Let Mister Beamish finish."

He sat down, looking like a mean dog waiting for the postman. Beamish ignored him. He went on, quietly,

"I have always held that entertainment, of the right sort, is the most valuable aid humanity can have in its search for the alleviation of toil and boredom...."

I said, "Sure, sure. But what was your idea?"

"There are many towns along the Venusian frontiers where no entertainment of the—*proper* sort has been available. I propose to remedy that. I propose to charter your circus, Mister Shannon, to make a tour of several settlements along the Tehara Belt."

Bucky had relaxed. His grey-green eyes began to gleam. He started to speak, and I kicked him again.

"That would be expensive, Mister Beamish," I said. "We'd have to cancel several engagements...."

He looked at me. I was lying, and he knew it. But he said,

"I quite understand that. I would be prepared...."

The curtains were yanked back suddenly. Beamish shut up. Bucky and I glared at the head and shoulders poking in between the drapes.

It was Gow, our zoo-man—a big, ugly son-of-a-gun from a Terran colony on Mercury. I was there once. Gow looks a lot like the scenery—scowling, unapproachable, and tough. His hands, holding the curtains apart, had thick black hair on them and were not much larger than the hams of a Venusian swamp-rhino.

He said, "Boss, Gertrude's actin' up again."

"Gertrude be blowed," growled Bucky. "Can't you see I'm busy?"

Gow's black eyes were unpleasant. "I'm tellin' you, Boss, Gertrude ain't happy. She ain't had the right food. If something...."

I said, "That'll all be taken care of, Gow. Run along now."

He looked at me like he was thinking it wouldn't take much timber to fit me for a coffin. "Okay! But Gertrude's unhappy. She's lonesome, see? And if she don't get happier pretty soon I ain't sure your tin-pot ship'll hold her."

He pulled the curtains to and departed. Bucky Shannon groaned. Beamish cleared his throat and said, rather stiffly,

"Gertrude?"

"Yeah. She's kind of temperamental." Bucky took a quick drink. I finished for him.

"She's the star attraction of our show, Mr. Beamish. A real blue-swamp Venusian *cansin*. The only other one on the Triangle belongs to Savitt Brothers, and she's much smaller than Gertrude."

She was also much younger, but I didn't go into that. Gertrude may be a little creaky, but she's still pretty impressive. I only hoped she wouldn't die on us, because without her we'd have a sicker-looking circus than even I could stand.

Beamish looked impressed. "A *cansin*. Well, well! The mystery surrounding the origin and species of the *cansin* is a fascinating subject. The extreme rarity of the animal...."

We were getting off the subject. I said tactfully, "We'd have to have at least a hundred U.C.'s."

It was twice what we had any right to ask. I was prepared to dicker. Beamish looked at me with that innocent dead pan. For a fraction of a second I thought I saw something back of his round blue eyes, and my stomach jumped like it was shot. Beamish smiled sweetly.

"I'm not much of a bargainer. One hundred Universal Credits will be agreeable to me." He dragged out a roll as big as my two fists, peeled off half a dozen credit slips, and laid them on the table.

"By way of a retainer, gentleman. My attorney and I will call on you in the morning with a contract and itinerary. Good night."

9

THE BLUE BEHEMOTH

We said good night, trying not to drool. Beamish went away. Bucky made grab for the money, but I beat him to it.

"Scram," I said. "There are guys waiting for this. Big guys with clubs. Here." I gave him a small-denomination slip I'd been holding out. "We can get lushed enough on this."

Shannon has a good vocabulary. He used it. When he got his breath back he said suddenly,

"Beamish is pulling some kind of a game."

"Yeah."

"It may be crooked."

"Sure. And he may be screwball and on the level. For Pete's sake!" I yelled. "You want to sit here till we all dry up and blow away?"

Shannon looked at me, kind of funny. He looked at the bulge in my tunic where the roll was. He raked back his thick light hair.

"Yeah," he said. "I hope there'll be enough left to bribe the jury." He poked his head outside. "Hey, boy! More *thildatum*!"

*

It was pretty late when we got back to the broken-down spaceport where Shannon's Imperial Circus was crouching beneath its attachments. Late as it was, they were waiting for us. About twenty of them, sitting around and smoking and looking very ugly.

It was awfully lonesome out there, with the desert cold and restless under the two moons. There's a smell to Mars, like something dead and dried long past decay, but still waiting. An unhappy smell. The blown red dust gritted in my teeth.

Bucky Shannon walked out into the glare of the light at the entrance to the roped-off space around the main lock. He was pretty steady on his feet. He waved and said, "Hiya, boys."

They got up off the steps, and the packing cases, and came toward us. I grinned and got into my brassies. We felt we owed those boys a

10

lot more than money. It grates on a man's pride to have to sneak in and out of his own property through the sewage lock. This was the first time in weeks we'd come in at the front door.

I waved the money in their faces. That stopped them. Very solemnly, Bucky and I checked the bills, paid them, and pocketed the receipts. Bucky yawned and stretched sleepily.

"Now?" he said.

"Now," I said.

We had a lot of fun. Some of the boys inside the ship came out to join in. We raised a lot of dust and nobody got killed, quite. We all went home happy. They had their money, and we had their blood.

The news was all over the ship before we got inside. The freaks and the green girl from Tethys who could roll herself like a hoop, and Zurt the muscle man from Jupiter, and all the other assorted geeks and kinkers and joeys that make up the usual corny carnie were doing nip-ups in the passageways and drooling over the thought of steer and toppings.

Bucky Shannon regarded them possessively, wiping blood from his nose. "They're good guys, Jig. Swell people. They stuck by me, and I've rewarded them."

I said, "Sure," rather sourly. Bucky hiccoughed.

"Let's go see Gertrude."

I didn't want to see Gertrude. I never got over feeling funny going into the brute tank, especially at night or out in space. I'm a city guy, myself. The smell and sound of wildness gives me goose bumps. But Bucky was looking stubborn, so I shrugged.

"Okay. But just for a minute. Then we go beddy-bye."

"You're a pal, Jif. Bes' li'l' guy inna worl'...."

11

THE BLUE BEHEMOTH

The fight had just put the topper on him. I was afraid he'd fall down the ladder and break his neck. That's why I went along. If I hadn't....Oh, well, what's a few nightmares among friends?

It was dark down there in the tank. Way off at the other end, there was a dim glow. Gow was evidently holding Gertrude's hand. We started down the long passageway between the rows of cages and glassed-in tanks and compression units.

Our footsteps sounded loud and empty on the iron floor. I wasn't near as happy as Shannon, and my skin began to crawl a little. It's the smell, I think; rank and sour and wild. And the sound of them, breathing and rustling in the dark, with the patient hatred walled around them as strong as the cage bars.

Bucky Shannon lurched against me suddenly. I choked back a yell, and then wiped the sweat off my forehead and cursed. The scream came again. A high, ragged, whistling screech like nothing this side of hell, ripping through the musty darkness. Gertrude, on the wailing wall.

It had been quiet. Now every brute in the place let go at the same time. My stomach turned clear over. I called Gertrude every name I could think of, and I couldn't hear myself doing it. Presently a great metallic clash nearly burst my eardrums, and the beasts shut up. Gow had them nicely conditioned to that gong.

*

But they didn't quiet down. Not really. They were uneasy. You can feel them inside you when they're uneasy. I think that's why I'm scared of them. They make me feel like I'm not human as I thought—like I wanted to put my back-hair up and snarl. Yeah. They were uneasy that night, all of a sudden....

Gow glared at us as we came up into the lantern light. "She's gettin' worse," he said. "She's lonesome."

LEIGH BRACKETT

"That's tough," said Bucky Shannon. His grey-green eyes looked like an owl's. He swayed slightly. "That's sure tough." He sniffled.

I looked at Gertrude. Her cage is the biggest and strongest in the tank and even so she looked as though she could break it open just taking a deep breath. I don't know if you've ever seen a *cansin*. There's only two of them on the Triangle. If you haven't, nothing I can say will make much difference.

They're what the brain gang calls an "end of evolution." Seems old Dame Nature had an idea that didn't jell. The *cansins* were pretty successful for a while, it seems, but something gummed up the works and now there's only a few left, way in the deep-swamp country, where even the Venusians hardly ever go. Living fossils.

I wouldn't know, of course, but Gertrude looks to me like she got stuck some place between a dinosaur and a grizzly bear, with maybe a little bird blood thrown in. Anyway, she's big.

I couldn't help feeling sorry for her. She was crouched in the cage with her hands—yeah, hands—hanging over her knees and her snaky head sunk into her shoulders, looking out. Just looking. Not at anything. Her eyes were way back in deep horny pits, like cold green fire.

The lantern light was yellow on her blue-black skin, but it made the mane, or crest, of coarse wide scales that ran from between her eyes clear down to her flat, short tail, burn all colors. She looked like old Mother Misery herself, from way back before time began.

Gow said softly, "She wants a mate. And somebody better get her one."

Bucky Shannon sniffled again. I said irritably, "Be reasonable, Gow! Nobody's ever seen a male *cansin*. There may not even be any."

Gertrude screamed again. She didn't move, not even to raise her head. The sadness just built up inside her until it had to come out.

13

THE BLUE BEHEMOTH

That close, the screech was deafening, and it turned me all limp and cold inside. The loneliness, the sheer stark, simple pain....

Bucky Shannon began to cry. I snarled, "You'll have to snap her out of this, Gow. She's driving the rest of 'em nuts."

He hammered on his gong, and things quieted down again. Gow stood looking out over the tank, sniffing a little, like a hound. Then he turned to Gertrude.

"I saved her life," he said. "When we bought her out of Hanak's wreck and everybody thought she was too hurt to live, I saved her. I know her. I can do things with her. But this time...."

He shrugged. He was huge and tough and ugly, and his voice was like a woman's talking about a sick child.

"This time," he said, "I ain't sure."

"Well for Pete's sake, do what you can. We got a charter, and we need her." I took Shannon's arm. "Come to bed, Bucky darlin'."

He draped himself over my shoulder and we went off. Gow didn't look at us. Bucky sobbed.

"You were right, Jig," he mumbled. "Circus is no good. I know it. But it's all I got. I love it, Jig. Unnerstan' me? Like Gow there with Gertrude. She's ugly and no good, but he loves her. I love...."

"Sure, sure," I told him. "Stop crying down my neck."

We were a long way from the light, then. The cages and tanks loomed high and black over us. It was still. The secret, uneasy motion all around us and the scruffing of our feet only made it stiller.

Bucky was almost asleep on me. I started to slap him. And then the mist rose up out of the darkness in little lazy coils, sparkling faintly with blue, cold fire.

I yelled, "Gow! Gow, the Vapor snakes! Gow—for God's sake!"

I started to run, back along the passageway. Bucky weighed on me, limp and heavy. The noise burst suddenly in a deafening hell of moans and roars and shrieks, packed in tight by the metal walls, and above it all I could hear Gertrude's lonely, whistling scream.

I thought, "*Somebody's down here. Somebody let 'em out. Somebody wants to kill us!*" I tried to yell again. It strangled in my throat. I sobbed, and the sweat was thick and cold on me.

One of Bucky's dragging, stumbling feet got between mine. We fell. I rolled on top of him, covering his face, and buried my own face in the hollow of his shoulder.

The first snake touched me. It was like a live wire, sliding along the back of my neck. I screamed. It came down along my cheek, hunting my mouth. There were more of them, burning me through my clothes.

Bucky moaned and kicked under me. I remember hanging on and thinking, "This is it. This is it, and oh God, I'm scared!"

Then I went out.

II

Kanza the Martian croaker, was bending over me when I woke up. His little brown face was crinkled with laughter. He'd lost most of his teeth, and he gummed *thak*-weed. It smelt.

"You pretty, Mis' Jig," he giggled. "You funny like hell."

He slapped some cold greasy stuff on my face. It hurt. I cursed him and said, "Where's Shannon? How is he?"

"Mis' Bucky okay. You save life. You big hero, Mis' Jig. Mis' Gow come nickuhtime get snakes. You hero. Haw! You funny like hell!"

I said, "Yeah," and pushed him away and got up. I almost fell down a couple of times, but presently I made it to the mirror over the washstand—I was in my own cell—and I saw what Kanza meant. The damned snakes had done a good job. I looked like I was upholstered in Scotch plaid. I felt sick.

Bucky Shannon opened the door. He looked white and grim, and there was a big burn across his neck. He said:

"Beamish is here with his lawyer."

I picked up my shirt. "Right with you."

Kanza went out, still giggling. Bucky closed the door.

"Jig," he said, "those vapor worms were all right when we went in. Somebody followed us down and let them out. On purpose."

I hurt all over. I growled, "With that brain, son, you should go far. Nobody saw anything, of course?" Bucky shook his head.

"Question is, Jig, who wants to kill us, and why?"

"Beamish. He realizes he's been gypped."

"One hundred U.C.'s," said Bucky softly, "for a few lousy swampedge mining camps. It stinks, Jig. You think we should back out?"

I shrugged. "You're the boss man. I'm only the guy that beats off the creditors."

THE BLUE BEHEMOTH

"Yeah," Bucky said reflectively. "And I hear starvation isn't a comfortable death. Okay, Jig. Let's go sign." He put his hand on the latch and looked at my feet. "And—uh—Jig, I...."

I said, "Skip it. The next time, just don't trip me up, that's all!"

We had a nasty trip to Venus. Gertrude kept the brute tank on edge, and Gow, on the rare occasions he came up for air, went around looking like a disaster hoping to happen. To make it worse, Zurt the Jovian strong-man got hurt during the take-off, and the Mercurian cave-cat had kittens.

Nobody would have minded that, only one of 'em had only four legs. It lived just long enough to scare that bunch of superstitious dopes out of their pants. Circus people are funny that way.

Shannon and I did a little quiet sleuthing, but it was a waste of time. Anybody in the gang might have let those electric worms out on us. It didn't help any to know that somebody, maybe the guy next to you at dinner, was busy thinking ways to kill you. By the time we hit Venus, I was ready to do a Brodie out the refuse chute.

Shannon set the crate down on the edge of Nahru, the first stop on our itinerary. I stood beside him, looking out the ports at the scenery. It was Venus, all right. Blue mud and thick green jungle and rain, and a bunch of ratty-looking plastic shacks huddling together in the middle of it. Men in slickers were coming out for a look.

I saw Beamish's sleek yacht parked on a cradle over to the left, and our router's runabout beside it. Bucky Shannon groaned.

"A blue one, Jig. A morgue if I ever saw one!"

I snarled, "What do you want, with this lousy dog-and-pony show!" and went out. He followed. The gang was converging on the lock, but they weren't happy. You get so you can feel those things. The steamy Venus heat was already sneaking into the ship.

18

While we passed the hatchway to the brute tank, I could hear Gertrude, screaming.

*

The canvasmen were busy setting up the annex, slopping and cursing in the mud. The paste brigade was heading for the shacks. Shannon and I stood with the hot rain running off our slickers, looking.

I heard a noise behind me and looked around. Ahra the Nahali woman was standing in the mud with her arms up and her head thrown back, and her triangular mouth open like a thirsty dog. She didn't have anything on but her blue-green, hard scaled hide, and she was chuckling. It didn't sound nice.

You find a lot of Nahali people in side-shows, doing tricks with the electric power they carry in their own bodies. They're Venusian middle-swampers, they're not human, and they never forget it.

Ahra opened her slitted red eyes and looked at me and laughed with white reptilian teeth.

"Death," she whispered. "Death and trouble. The jungle tells me. I can smell it in the swamp wind."

The hot rain sluiced over her. She shivered, and the pale skin under her jaw pulsed like a toad's, and her eyes were red.

"The deep swamps are angry," she whispered. "Something has been taken. They are angry, and I smell death in the wind!"

She turned away, laughing, and I cursed her, and my stomach was tight and cold. Bucky said,

"Let's eat if they have a bar in this dump."

We weren't half way across the mud puddle that passed as a landing field when a man came out of a shack on the edge of the settlement. We could see him plainly, because he was off to one side of the crowd.

THE BLUE BEHEMOTH

He fell on his knees in the mud, making noises. It took him three or four tries to get our names out clear enough to understand.

Bucky said, "Jig—it's Sam Kapper."

We started to run. The crowd, mostly big unshaken miners, wheeled around to see what was happening. People began to close in on the man who crawled and whimpered in the mud.

Sam Kapper was a hunter, supplying animals to zoos and circuses and carnivals. He'd given us good deals a couple of times, when we weren't too broke, and we were pretty friendly.

I hadn't seen him for three seasons. I remembered him as a bronzed, hard-bitten guy, lean and tough as a twist of tung wire. I felt sick, looking down at him.

Bucky started to help him up. Kapper was crying, and he jerked all over like animals I've seen that were scared to death. Some guy leaned over and put a cigarette in his mouth and lighted it for him.

I was thinking about Kapper, then, and I didn't pay much attention. I only caught a glimpse of the man's face as he straightened up. I didn't realize until later that he looked familiar.

We got Kapper inside the shack. It turned out to be a cheap bar, with a couple of curtained booths at the back. We got him into one and pulled the curtain in a lot of curious faces. Kapper dragged hard on the cigarette. The man that gave it to him was gone.

Bucky said gently, "Okay, Sam. Relax. What's the trouble?"

*

Kapper tried to straighten up. He hadn't shaved. The lean hard lines of his face had gone slack and his eyes were bloodshot. He was covered with mud, and his mouth twitched like a sick old man's.

He said thickly, "I found it. I said I'd do it, and I did. I found it and brought it out."

20

The cigarette stub fell out of his mouth. He didn't notice it. "Help me," he said simply. "I'm scared." His mouth drooled.

"I got it hidden. They want to find out, but I won't tell 'em. It's got to go back. Back where I found it. I tried to take it, but they wouldn't let me, and I was afraid they'd find it...."

He reached suddenly and grabbed the edge of the table. "I don't know how they found out about it, but they did. I've got to get it back. I've got to...."

Bucky looked at me. Kapper was blue around the mouth. I was scared, suddenly. I said, "Get what back where?"

Bucky got up. "I'll get a doctor," he said. "Stick with him." Kapper grabbed his wrist. Kapper's nails were blue and the cords in his hands stood out like guy wires.

"Don't leave me. Got to tell you—where it is. Got to take it back. Promise you'll take it back." He gasped and struggled over his breathing.

"Sure," said Bucky. "Sure, well take it back. What is it?"

Kapper's face was horrible. I felt sick, listening to him fight for air. I wanted to go for a doctor anyway, but somehow I knew it was no use. Kapper whispered,

"*Cansin.* Male. Only one. You don't know...! Take him back."

"Where is it, Sam?"

I reached across Bucky suddenly and jerked the curtain back. Beamish was standing there. Beamish, bent over, with his ear cocked. Kapper made a harsh strangling noise and fell across the table.

Beamish never changed expression. He didn't move while Bucky felt Kapper's pulse. Bucky didn't need to say anything. We knew.

"Heart?" said Beamish finally.

"Yeah," said Bucky. He looked as bad as I felt. "Poor Sam."

THE BLUE BEHEMOTH

I looked at the cigarette stub smoldering on the table. I looked at Beamish with his round dead baby face. I climbed over Shannon and pushed Beamish suddenly down into his lap.

"Keep this guy here till I get back," I said.

Shannon stared at me. Beamish started to get indignant. "Shut up," I told him. "We got a contract." I yanked the curtains shut and walked over to the bar.

I began to notice something, then. There were quite a lot of men in the place. At first glance they looked okay—a hard-faced, muscular bunch of miners in dirty shirts and high boots.

Then I looked at their hands. They were dirty enough. But they never did any work in a mine, on Venus or anywhere else.

The place was awfully quiet, for that kind of a place. The bartender was a big pot-bellied swamp-edger with pale eyes and thick white hair coiled up on top of his bullet head. He was not happy.

I leaned on the bar. "*Lhak*," I said. He poured it, sullenly, out of a green bottle. I reached for it, casually.

"That guy we brought in," I said. "He sure has a skinful. Passed out cold. What's he been spiking his drinks with?"

"*Selak*," said a voice in my ear. "As if you didn't know."

I turned. The man who had given Kapper the cigarette was standing behind me. And I remembered him, then.

*

Circus people get around a lot, and the Law supplies us with Wanted sheets. I remembered this guy from the last batch they handed us on Mars. Melak Thompson was his name, and he had a reputation.

He had a face you wouldn't forget. Dark and kind of handsome, with the Dry-lander blood showing in the heavy bones and the tilted green eyes. His mouth was smiling and brutal. He nodded at the booth.

"Let's take a walk," he said.

We took a walk. The men sitting at the dirty tables were still silent, and still not miners. I began to sweat.

The booth was a little crowded with us all in there. I sat jammed up against Sam Kapper's body. Bucky Shannon's grey-green eyes were sleepy, and there was a vein beating on his forehead.

Beamish said to Melak, "Kapper's dead. Dead, without talking."

"That's tough." Melak shook his dark head. "We was gentle with him."

"Yeah," I said. Kapper had been a good guy, and I was mad. "Feed anybody enough *selak*, and you can afford to be. It's a dirty death."

Selak's made from a Venusian half-cousin of henbane, which is what scopolamine comes from. It has a terrific effect on the heart. And Kapper had simply torn himself apart trying to keep from talking while he was under the influence.

Bucky Shannon made a slow, ugly move to get up. Beamish said, "Sit down."

There was something in his voice and his bland blue eyes. Shannon sat down. Melak was looking at Beamish, still grinning.

"Well," he said, "I guess your idea was pretty good after all."

I had a sudden inspiration. The burns were still sore on my body, and Rapper's tortured face was close to mine, and I took a wild shot at something I wasn't even sure I saw.

"Yeah," I said. "A swell idea. Why did you try so hard to butch it, Melak?"

He stopped grinning. Beamish looked forward a little. My tongue stuck in my mouth, but I managed to say.

THE BLUE BEHEMOTH

"You get it, Bucky. A male *cansin*, Kapper said. The only one in captivity, maybe even on Venus. Worth its weight in credit slips. That's why Beamish was so happy to overpay us to get us out here—because he thought Gertrude could find her boy friend fast, even if Kapper didn't talk."

I turned to Melak again. "A swell idea. Why did you have those vapor snakes turned loose on us? Did you think Kapper was enough?"

He struck me, pretty hard, across the mouth. My head banged back against the booth wall and for a minute I couldn't see anything but spangles of fire shooting around. I heard Beamish say, from a great distance,

"How about it, Melak?"

It was awfully still in the booth. I swallowed some blood and blinked my eyes clear enough to see Bucky Shannon poised across the table like a bow starting to unbend. And suddenly, somewhere far off over the drum of rain on the flimsy roof, there began to be noises.

I hadn't been comfortable up till then. I'm no Superman, nor one of those guys you read about who can stare Death in the eye and shatter him with a light laugh.

But all of a sudden I was afraid. Afraid so that all the fear I'd felt before was nothing. And it was funny, too. I didn't know what it was, then, but I knew what it wasn't. It wasn't Beamish or Melak or those hard guys beyond the curtains, or even Kapper's body pressed up against me.

I didn't know what it was. But I wanted to get down on the floor and hide myself in a crack, like a cockroach.

*

The others felt it, too. I remember the sweat standing out on Bucky Shannon's forehead, and the sudden tightening of Beamish's jaw, and the glitter in Melak's green eyes.

24

Beyond the curtains there was an uneasy stirring of feet. The confused, distant noise grew louder. Somewhere, not very far away, a woman began to scream.

Beamish said softly, "You dirty double-crossing rat." His face was still dead-pan, only now it was like something beaten out of iron. His hands were out of sight under the table.

Melak smiled. I could feel his body shift and tense beside me. "Sure," he said. "I double-crossed you. Why not? I planted a guy in the circus hammer gang and he crawled in the sewage lock and tried to get these punks. I'm glad now he bungled it. Kapper had guts."

Beamish whispered, "You're a fool. You don't know what you're playing with. I've done research, and I do."

"Too bad you wasted the time," said Melak. "Because you're through."

He threw himself suddenly aside, lifting the table hard into Beamish. The curtains ripped away and he rolled in them, twisting like a snake. I yelled to Bucky and dropped flat. Beamish had drawn a gun under the table. The blast of it seared my face.

The next second four heavy blasters spoke at once. Beamish's gun dropped on the floor. Then it was quiet again, and I could hear the woman screaming, outside in the beating rain.

Melak got up. "Sure I double-crossed you," he said softly. "Why should I split with anybody? Nobody knows about it but us. Kapper couldn't send word from the swamps when he caught it, and he couldn't send word from here because he wasn't let.

"That critter'll bring anything I ask for it. Why should I split with you?"

Beamish didn't answer. I don't think Melak thought he would.

The noise from outside was getting louder. Bucky groaned.

"It's coming from the pitch, Jig. Trouble. We've got to...."

THE BLUE BEHEMOTH

The table was yanked from over us. We got up off our knees. Melak looked at us. He was shaking a little and his green eyes were mean.

"I don't think," he said, "I really need you guys around, either." He jerked his head suddenly. "Cripes, I wish that dame would shut up!"

It was getting on my nerves, too—that monotonous, sawing screech. Melak stepped aside. "Get 'em, boys. I don't want 'em dragging their outfit down on our necks."

Four blaster barrels came up. My insides came up with them. I was way beyond anything, then—even panic.

Gow burst in through the doorway.

He was soaked to the skin, tattered, bleeding, and wild-eyed. He yelled, "Boss! Gertrude...." Then he saw the guns and stopped.

It was very still in the place. Outside there was sound rising like a sullen tide against the walls. The woman's screaming became something not human, and then stopped, short.

Gow said, almost absently, "Gertrude went nuts. We'd brought her cage up from the tank for the show and she—broke out. There wasn't nothin' we could do. She busted a lot of cages and then disappeared."

Melak snarled something, I don't know what. The wall behind Gow jarred, buckled, and split open around the doorway. Bamboo fragments clattered on the floor. Somebody yelled, and a blaster went off.

Gertrude stood in the splintered opening. She looked at us with cold, mad green eyes, towering huge and blue against the low roof, her hands swinging and her crest erect.

She let go one wild, whistling screech and came straight toward the booth. Bucky Shannon touched my arm.

"Climb into your brassies, kid," he muttered. "Here's our chance!"

I caught his shoulder. He followed the line of my pointing, and I felt him tremble.

Gertrude was coming at us like a rocket express. Behind her wet and glistening from the hot rain, came three more just like her.

III

We scattered, all of us, hunting for a way out. There was only one door leading to the back, and it was stoppered tight with men cursing and fighting to get through. Gow was crouched in a corner by the splintered wall.

I pulled Bucky along, thinking we might get in back of the *cansins* and sneak out. I wondered what they wanted. And I wondered where in heck you could hide a thing as big as Gertrude and keep anybody from finding out.

Somebody screamed briefly. I saw one of the strange *cansins* toss the bartender aside like a dry twig. Gow rose up in front of me with a queer staring look in his eyes.

"Somethin's wrong," he said. "All wrong. I...." His mouth twitched. He turned sharply and started to scramble through the wrecked hall. Bucky and I were right on his heels. I think Melak and some of his lobbygows were crowding us, but nobody was thinking about things like that any more.

I knew what was eating Gow. The fear that had looked out of Kapper's eyes. The fear that was riding me. Fear that had nothing to do with anything physical.

Bucky cursed and stumbled beside me. And suddenly the four *cansins* let go a tremendous thundering scream. The hair rose on my neck, and I turned to look. I just had to.

Gertrude had turned away from the booth. They stood, the four of them, their huge black shoulders touching, their crests like rows of petrified flame, staring at what Gertrude held in her arms.

It was Kapper's body.

Slowly, with infinite gentleness, she began to strip him. He hung loose in the cradle of one great arm, his flesh showing blue-white against her blueness. Her free hand ripped his clothes away like things made of paper.

I don't know why nobody tried to shoot the beasts after the first second. Sheer panic, I guess. We could have killed them all, then. But we just stood looking, fascinated by the slow, intent baring of Kapper's body.

And the strange fear. It was on us all.

Kapper lay naked in her black arms. She raised him slowly over her head, her eyes blind green fires deep under bony brows. The others drew closer, shivering, and I could hear them whimper.

Strangers from the deep swamps with no stink of man on them. I thought of the Nahali woman laughing in the hot rain. Death from the deep swamps, because something had been taken, and they were angry.

There was a little black box strapped to Kapper's thin white belly.

Gertrude shifted her hands a little. The blood hammered in my ears. I was sick. I didn't want to look any more. I couldn't help it. Bucky Shannon caught a hard, sobbing breath.

Gertrude broke Sam Kapper's body in two.

*

I can still hear the noise it made. The blood ran dark and sluggish down her arms. It worried me that Kapper's face didn't change expression. The little black box on his belly split with the rest of him.

Something rose out of it. Something no bigger than my forefinger that carried a cold green blaze around it like a ball of St. Elmo's fire.

Gertrude threw Kapper away. I heard the two flopping thuds of him hitting the floor. Some guy was down on his knees close to me. His lips moved. I don't know if he could remember his prayers. Somebody else was vomiting, hard. I wanted to, but my stomach felt frozen.

LEIGH BRACKETT

The cold green fire had a shape inside it. I couldn't make it out clearly, except that it looked horribly human. It put out four thin green filaments. Don't ask me if they were physical things like tentacles, or just beams of light, or maybe thought. I don't know. Whatever they were, they worked.

They connected with the four black, snaky heads of the female *cansins*. I felt the shock of them connecting with my own nerves. And it was like something had welded those four brutes together into one.

They had been four. Separate, with hard outlines. Now they were one. One single interlocking entity. I guess it was just my being so scared and sick, but I thought I saw their outlines blur a little.

Gow spoke suddenly. His voice was pretty loud, and calm.

"That was it," he said, as though it was the only thing in the world that mattered. "They ain't complete by themselves. Like the *zurats* back home on Mercury. They got a community brain. No wonder Gertrude was lonesome."

His voice broke the spell. Somebody screamed, and everybody started to move at once, clawing in blind panic for the openings. And we all knew, then, what we were afraid of.

We were afraid of the little thing in the black box, the thing in a cloak of fire that had risen from the ruins of Kapper's body, and the power that lived in it.

I suppose we thought we were going to fight it, all right. But outside, where we could breathe. Not in here, with the hugeness of the females smothering us, penned in with the last male *cansin* in creation.

I knew then why Kapper had broken, and why he hadn't told, in spite of the *selak*. The thing hadn't let him. And it had called to its kind, from the deep swamps and Buckhalter Shannon's Imperial Circus.

*

The deep indigo night of Venus had settled down, in the smell of mud and jungle and the hot rain. Lights flared crazily here and there out of open doorways. People were yelling, the tight, animal mob-yell of fear.

There was no place to run in Nahru. The jungle held it. The thick green jungle built on quicksand and crawling with death. Behind us the four *cansins* raised a wild whistling screech.

It was answered, out of the hot night between the little shacks of Nahru. Brute voices, singing their hate. Suddenly I remembered what Gow had said. *"She busted a lot of cages...."*

God knew what was loose in that town.

Bucky Shannon spoke beside me. We were still running, slipping and floundering in the mud, making toward the ship from sheer instinct. He gasped,

"We got to get those babies rounded up. Gow! Gow, you hear me? We got to get 'em back!"

Gow's voice came sullenly. "I hear you, boss." We slowed down. It was suddenly important to hear what more Gow had to say.

"Don't you get it?" he asked slowly. "Gertrude let 'em out. She wanted 'em—to help her. They know it. They ain't going back."

Somewhere behind us a plastic shack cracked open like an eggshell. Human cries were drowned in a whistling screech. Off to the right the Mercurian cave-cat began to laugh like a crazy woman.

Slow, patient, animal hate, walled around them, waiting. The feel and smell of hate in the brute tank. I could feel and smell it now, in Nahru, only it wasn't patient and waiting any more.

The time it had waited for was here. Gertrude had set it free.

32

Shannon said, very softly, "Mother o' God, what are we going to do?"

"Get back to the ship. Get back and get out of here!"

I jumped. It was Melak's voice, sounding hard and ugly. Light spilling out of a sagging door made a faint silhouette of him in the rain. He held a blaster in his hand.

Shannon snarled, "Take off with half my gang stranded here? You go to hell!"

Rockets blasted suddenly out on the landing field. Somebody had made it to Beamish's yacht and gone. The runabout followed it. The circus ship was still there, and the only one in Nahru.

I said, "We can't go. Not with a couple hundred credits' worth of animals running loose in the town."

"Get on to the ship," said Melak. "Cripes, if I knew how to fly I'd leave you here! Now move!"

Shannon was almost crying. He started to rush Melak. I caught him and said, "Sure. Sure we'll move. All of us. Look behind you!"

"I was weaned on that one. Move!"

Well, it was his funeral.

*

It was almost ours, too. Ganymedian puffballs move fast. They had come out from between two shacks, skimming over the mud on their long white cilia. There were three of them, rolled up in balls about the size of my head. They didn't make any noise.

They came up behind Melak. Two of them unrolled suddenly, whipping out into lean, fuzzy ropes about five feet long. They went around the Martian breed. The third one came straight at me.

Melak made a noise that wasn't human and went down. The puffballs tightened around him, pulsing a little with the pleasure of digestion. Gow was on the other side of Melak, too far away, and unarmed.

I jumped, and the mud tripped me. Shannon fell the other way. The puffball, strung out now like a fuzzy snake, paused a moment, not three inches from my face. I lay still on my belly, choking on my heart.

Shannon moved, and it whipped down across his legs.

He screamed. I could feel the poison from the thing eating into him. I got to my knees and he cursed me and raised something out of the mud. It was Melak's blaster. He fired, between his feet.

The puffball shrivelled to a little stinking wire and dropped away. Bucky said evenly,

"That pays me off. Now it's all your party, Jig."

He fainted. His legs were already swelling. Gow bent over him.

"He's gotta have the croaker, quick."

"You take him to the ship, Gow. If you can get there."

"Me? I'm the zoo-man. I oughta...."

"Do I look like Superman, to carry that big lug?" I didn't know why it was so hard to talk. "Get him there. Then round up everybody left at the ship. Get guns and ropes and torches and come back, quick!"

He nodded and got Bucky across his shoulders. I gave him the blaster. Then I turned back. I knew where most of the circus gang would be—spread out among the bars.

It was a lot darker, because now all the doors were closed, except two or three where the people hadn't lived to close them. It was quieter, too, because there's a limit to the noise a human throat can make. There was just the hot rain, and the soft jungle undertone of things padding and slithering in the mud, hunting.

Up the street somewhere the *cansins* screamed, and another shack split open. Instantly the brute clamor went up from the dark alleys, answering. Animal legions from five different planets, led by a tiny creature in a cloak of green fire. And man was the common enemy.

A pair of Martian sand-tigers shot out into the street ahead of me. They were frolicking like kittens, playing with something dark and tattered. Then they saw me and dropped it, and came sliding on their bellies, their six powerful legs sucking in the mud.

There was no place to go. I don't remember being particularly scared, but that wasn't because I was brave. It was sheer exhaustion. A guy can only take so much. Now I was just walking around, seeing and hearing, but not feeling anything inside. Like a guy that's coked to the ears, or punchy from a beating.

I picked up a double handful of mud and slung it in their snarling pusses, and threw my head back and yelled.

"Ha-a-y *Rube!*"

A door at my left opened three inches, daggering the rain with yellow light. A voice said,

"For gossakes get in here!"

I picked up another handful of mud. The Martian cats were pawing the last load out of their eyes. I gave them more to play with. I guess they weren't very hungry, just then. I said,

"I'm going to get the *cansins.*"

Just like that. I told you I was out on my feet. Clean nuts. The guy in the doorway thought so too.

"Will you come in before you're too dead?"

"And wait around for those big apes to crack the house open over my head? The hell with that." More mud sploshed in the cats' faces. They were beginning to get sore. "The rest of the critters are just following the *cansins.* Sort of a mopping-up brigade. Stop the *cansins,* and we can round up the others easy."

THE BLUE BEHEMOTH

"Oh, sure," said the man. "Any time before breakfast. Are you coming, pal, or do I shut this door again?"

I don't know how it would have turned out. Probably I'd have wound up inside the cats. But one of 'em let out a shrill, nasty wail, the kind they give the trainer when they're challenging him to a finish fight, and somebody came shouldering out past the man in the doorway.

The door swung wide, so that there was plenty of light. The six-inch fangs on the Martian kitties were a beautiful, shining white. The newcomer said something to the cats in a level undertone and came to me.

It was Jarin, the Titan who works the cats. He's about half my height, metallic green in color, and faster on his feet than a rummy grabbing the first drink. He looks like a walking barrel when he's folded up, and like nothing on earth when he isn't.

He was unfolded then. He went up to the cats, light and dainty in the mud. They were crouching uneasily, coughing and snarling, wanting to rush him and not quite daring to.

The male sprang.

IV

All I could see was a green blur in the rain. I heard the crisp, wicked smacks of Jarin's tentacles on the tiger. It flopped over in mid-air, buried its face in the mud and came up yowling, like your Aunt Minnie's cat when you stepped on its tail.

It went away from there, fast, with its mate right behind it.

Jarin chuckled softly. "About the *cansins*," he hissed. "You had an idea?"

Somewhere, quite close to us, there was the familiar sound of a plastic shack going to pieces. I remembered hearing blasters rip occasionally. But only Melak's hoods were armed with anything heavy enough to do any good, and I guessed most of them had beat it to Beamish's yacht. A *cansin* has a hell of a tough hide, and their vitality is something you wouldn't believe if you hadn't seen it.

The familiar whistling screech went up, and the babel of human screams and the brute chorus from the rainy alleys. I think, right then, I began to get scared. The fear began to seep through my dopey calm, like pain in a new wound.

I shuddered and said, "No. No ideas."

There was a soft step in the mud behind me. I spun around, sweating. Ahra the Nahali woman stood there, red-eyed and laughing.

"You are frightened," she whispered.

I didn't deny it.

"I can help you stop the *cansins*." Her eyes glittered like wet rubies, and her teeth were white and sharp. "It may not work, and you may die. Will you try it?"

She was daring me. She was hardly more human than the brutes themselves, and she belonged with the rain and the hot indigo night.

I said, "You don't want to help, Ahra. You want us to die."

THE BLUE BEHEMOTH

I could see the pale skin throbbing under her bony jaw. She laughed, soft alien laughter that made my back hair stir and prickle.

"You humans," she whispered. "Trampling and spoiling. The middle swamps have suffered you, greedy after oil and plumes and *ti*. But you we can fight."

She jerked her round, glistening head toward the sound of destruction. "The death from the deep swamps, no. You deserve to die, you humans. You went meddling with something too big even for your pride. But because the *cansins* killed my mate and our first young...."

She hunched up. I thought she was going to flop on her belly like a cayman in the mud. Her teeth gleamed, sharp and savage.

"Legend says the *cansins* were once the wisest race on Venus. They were worshipped as gods by the little pre-human creatures of the swamp edges. They were going to be the reasoning lords of a planet.

"But nature made a mistake. Perhaps some mutation that couldn't be stopped. I don't know. Anyway, the females grew until their one thought was to find enough food. The males tried to balance this. Most of their strength was in their minds, anyway. But they couldn't.

"The *cansins* took to eating their worshippers. At the same time the number of eggs they laid grew smaller and smaller. Finally the swamp-edgers drove them out, back into the deep swamps.

"They've been there ever since, going farther and farther on the path of evolution, dwindling in numbers, always hungry, and hating the humans who robbed them of their future. Even us they hate, because we go erect and have speech. The females are not independent. The male controls the community mind—they must have unity to exist at all.

"If you could control the male...."

38

I thought of the little creature in the ball of green fire. I shivered, and the pit of my stomach pinched up. I said, "Yeah? How?"

She chuckled at me. "It may mean death. Will you risk it?"

I didn't have to. I could beat it back to the ship, maybe even rescue some of the gang, with Jarin's help. Then I thought about Bucky and the way he cried down my neck that night in the tank and what would happen to us if we didn't get the animals rounded up. I thought—oh, hell, why does a guy ever do anything? I don't know. Maybe I thought I'd never get across the field to the ship anyhow.

I said, "Spill it, you she-snake. What do I do?"

"Get Quern," she said, and went off through the hot rain, back into the plastic shack. The door slammed shut. Jarin and I were alone in the dark.

I said, "Will you help me?"

"Of course."

I looked down the street toward the landing field. I felt tired, suddenly. Gone in the knees and weak, and sick to vomiting with fear.

"Here comes Gow," I said. "He's got seven or eight guys with guns. Just keep the critters off us until we get through with the *cansins*, and try not to kill any more than you can help."

Good old Jig, thinking about money even then. Gow came up. We talked a minute, just the things that had to be said, and then I asked,

"Anybody have an idea where Quern might be?"

"Yeah," said Gow slowly. "He was in the ginmill next to the one we was in. Drunk. I heard him singin' when I went by. I think the big apes wrecked it."

*

We started off up the muddy street, more as though we'd been wound up to go somewhere and couldn't stop than like men with a

39

purpose. The *cansins* were close. Awful close. You could hear them sucking and slopping in the muck. The rain fell straight down, almost solid, and the air was thick and hot.

We did a lot of shouting. Some men came out of the shacks to join us, but nobody had seen Quern since the trouble started. We had trouble with the animals in the streets. The vapor snakes got one man, and an Ionian *hru* poisoned one guy so bad he died the next day. We had to kill a couple of big babies that wouldn't scare off.

And we found the ginmill. Gow was right. It was wrecked, and there were things scattered around amongst the splinters. I was glad it was dark.

"Well," I said, "that's that. We'll just have to do what we can with the blasters." It wouldn't be much. We didn't carry any heavy artillery, and a *cansin* is awfully hard to stop.

"Any you guys wanta scram, do it now. The rest of you come on."

I took a step. Something squirmed under my foot, squeaked, and began to curse in a voice like a katydid's.

"My God," I said. "It's Quern."

I picked him up. His rubbery little body was slick with mud. He spat and hiccoughed, and snarled,

"Of course it's Quern. Fine thing, leaving me in the mud like that. I might ha' drowned." He started cursing again in Low Martian, which is his native tongue. He's a Diran from the sea-bottom pits of Shun.

Somebody laughed. It sounded hysterical. "The little lush! He don't even know what's happened!"

And he didn't. The *cansins* hadn't even seen him. He'd just been tromped into the mud and left there, unharmed.

Gow caught his breath suddenly, and somebody whimpered. I looked up. I couldn't see much, in the rain and the indigo dark, but I didn't have to see. I knew what was coming.

A little vicious splotch of living green against the darkness, and underneath it four huge shadows, trampling knee-deep in mud, making toward a plastic hut filled with human beings.

I said softly, "Quern, I never thought you were such a hell of a wonderful hypnotist."

He twinged in my hands. His anger almost burned me. He started to speak, but I stopped him.

"Here's your chance to prove it, chum. See that little green light floating there? Well, go to it, Quern. And it had better be good, or it's curtains—for Nahru and all of us."

I walked over toward the *cansins*, holding Quern in my hands.

*

The brutes must have sensed us. They stopped and wheeled around. Quern shivered. He was beginning to understand things. He snarled,

"How do you expect me to do my act? No platform—nothing! You're crazy, Jig! Let's get out of here!"

I shook him. "Put that baby to sleep. Make him and his harem go out of town, north. There's quicksand there. Go on, damn you!"

He cursed me. You could smell the fear rising hot from us all. I heard feet running behind me, and then more, going away. Quern said,

"All right, you crazy fool. Raise me up. Hold your hands flat."

I made a platform out of my palms. And the *cansins* started our way.

THE BLUE BEHEMOTH

Gow whispered, "Don't shoot. Don't anybody shoot." I don't think he knew then, that there wasn't anybody left to shoot but himself and Jarin.

The *cansins* were huge and solid, behemoths carved from the night. They towered over us, and the green light pulsed. My jaw hung open and I couldn't breathe, and I'd have run only my joints were all water.

Quern went into his act.

He began to show color. Out of nothing his body started to glow, from inside. You could see the round blurred shape of him, and the phosphorescence of his guts, showing through. First red, savage as a punch in the face, and then all the rest of the spectrum, sometimes one color, sometimes a swirl of them.

His body changed shape. I could feel the queer rubbery movement of it on my hands. I remembered the rubes I'd seen standing around Quern's platform, their eyes drawn half out of their heads by the shifting lines and colors. It worked with them. But not here.

The *cansins* came on. The green light flared a little brighter, and that was all. Habit and control were so strong that not even the females paid much attention to Quern. I could see the rain smoking off their huge black shoulders. They were right on top of us.

Quern gasped, "I can't do it!" His glow deadened. I shook him. I yelled,

"I knew you were a phony! You two-bit yentzer! Jarin, slow 'em down, can't you?"

Quern began to shimmer again. Jarin faded in, hardly visible in the darkness. I heard his tentacles whiplashing across hard flesh.

One of the *cansins* screamed. The green light did a sharp dip and swirl. And I yelled,

"Gow! Speak to Gertrude!"

The terrifying forward march slowed a little. Quern was churning colors out of his guts as though his life depended on it—which it did. Gow stepped forward a little.

"Gertrude," he said. "Gertrude, you ugly, slab-sided, left-handed—"

He cursed her, affectionately. I never heard anything like his voice. I wanted to cry. In Quern's faint hypnotic glow I saw the green eyes of the nearest female watching, looking wide and queer.

The male was angry, now. Angry and scared. You could tell by the vicious brightness of him. We decided afterward that his light was the same kind a glow-worm carries around, only stronger. He was fighting. Fighting to hold those four minds against the attraction of Quern's shifting glow.

He'd have done it, too, if it hadn't been for Gow. Gow, standing in the hot rain and cursing Gertrude with tears in his voice.

Gertrude screamed. Suddenly, for no reason, a strange uncertain cry. She moved. A sort of shudder ran through the other three. It was a little like a wall cracking. The male burned savagely.

The females were watching Quern, now. Gertrude had made the breach. Now the community mind was fastened on the hypnotic little Martian. I could see their green eyes, wide and glassy, their snaky heads nodding a little, trying to follow the flowing outlines.

The male began to dim. He shivered, and lurched a couple of times, still trying to fight. Gow's voice went on, hoarsely, and Gertrude whimpered. The male floated a little closer. I could see, suddenly, what kept him up. Wings, like a hummingbird's, blurred with motion.

They slowed, and the green light dimmed. He began to bob a little in the hot rain, watching Quern.

Quern shivered. "They're under," he sighed. "They're under."

THE BLUE BEHEMOTH

"Send them out. North, to the quicksands." My arms and shoulders ached and I was swaying on my feet. I hardly heard Quern's thin, dreamy voice. I did hear the slow, obedient noise of their great feet slogging away, the last male *cansin* a dull green mote above them.

And I heard Gow crying.

*

We got the last of the animals back by noon of the next day. We did what we could for Nahru. Thank God our own beasts hadn't done much damage. We left a lot of Beamish's credits to help out, and took the old tub off away from there.

Bucky Shannon recovered nicely. I'm still herding his Imperial Washout around the Triangle. We're not doing so hot without Gertrude, but what the hell—we're used to the sewage lock.

And if anyone has a *cansin* he wants to sell....Thanks, chum, but we're not in the market. Now, or ever.

I sometimes wonder if there are any more of them in the deep swamps, waiting for their mate to come back.